BUILT *for* BATTLE

AIRCRAFT CARRIERS

Valerie Bodden

CREATIVE 🍎 EDUCATION

Published by Creative Education
P.O. Box 227, Mankato, Minnesota 56002
Creative Education is an imprint of The Creative Company
www.thecreativecompany.us

Design and production by Liddy Walseth
Art direction by Rita Marshall
Printed by Corporate Graphics in the United States of America

Photographs by Corbis (Bettmann, George Hall), Defense Imagery (MC3 Oliver Cole,
LCDR Slowik, MC1 Scott Taylor, MC2 Gina K. Wollman), Getty Images (Check Six,
Alta I. Cutler/US Navy, Dorling Kindersley, Science Faction), iStockphoto (Chris Downie,
Chris Evans, Tobias Helbig, Andrew Howe, Sambrogio, James Steidl, Chad Thomas)

Library of Congress Cataloging-in-Publication Data

Bodden, Valerie.
Aircraft carriers / by Valerie Bodden.
Includes bibliographical references and index.
Summary: A fundamental exploration of aircraft carriers, including their size and carrying capacity,
history of development, flight decks and other features, and famous models from around the world.
ISBN 978-1-60818-122-3
1. Aircraft carriers—Juvenile literature. I. Title.
V874.B64 2011
623.825'5—dc22 2010053673

CPSIA: 112612 PO1620

4 6 8 9 7 5 3

BUILT for BATTLE

AIRCRAFT
CARRIERS

Valerie Bodden

TABLE OF
contents

A huge ship floats on the ocean. It is big enough to hold 85 airplanes and a runway!

Thousands of people live and work on the ship.

This is an aircraft carrier!

Aircraft carriers are ships that airplanes and helicopters can take off from and land on. Aircraft carriers PATROL oceans. They send airplanes out to fight enemies. The fastest aircraft carriers can move through the water at 40 miles (64 km) per hour.

An aircraft carrier crew member directing planes to take off

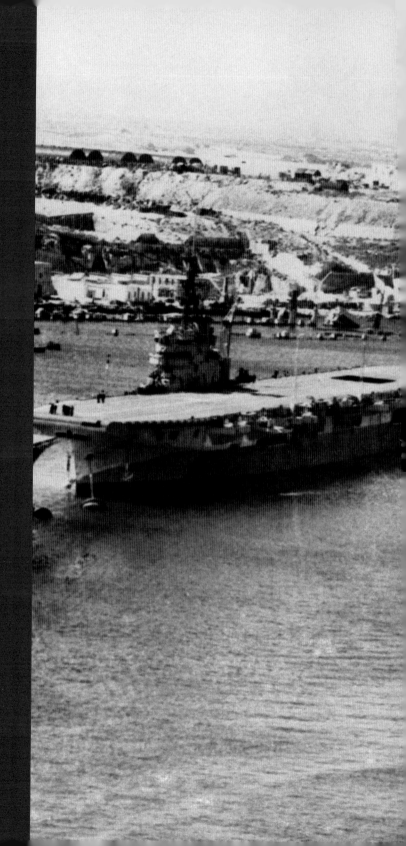

Famous Aircraft Carrier
Colossus Class

COUNTRY

Great Britain

ENTERED SERVICE

1944

LENGTH

695 feet (212 m)

WIDTH

80 feet (24.4 m)

WEIGHT

13,190 tons (11,966 t)

FASTEST SPEED

29 miles (47 km) per hour

CREW

1,300

Colossus aircraft carriers were small and light, so they could be built quickly. They could carry 48 airplanes. This was more than many other aircraft carriers of the 1940s could carry.

Aircraft first began to take off from ships in 1910. The first aircraft carriers were other types of warships with platforms added as runways. Soon, huge ships were being built just to carry aircraft.

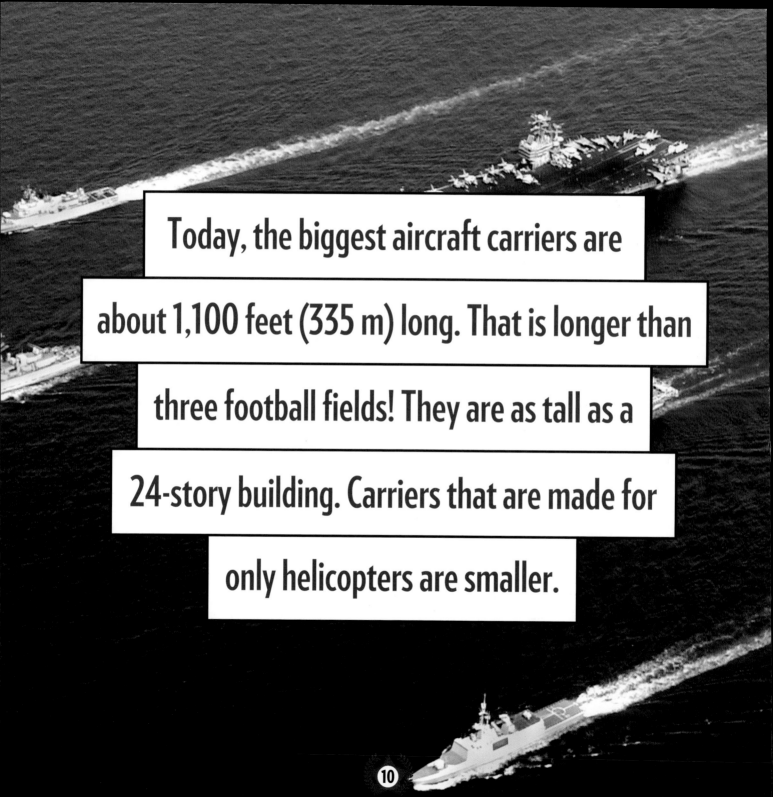

Today, the biggest aircraft carriers are about 1,100 feet (335 m) long. That is longer than three football fields! They are as tall as a 24-story building. Carriers that are made for only helicopters are smaller.

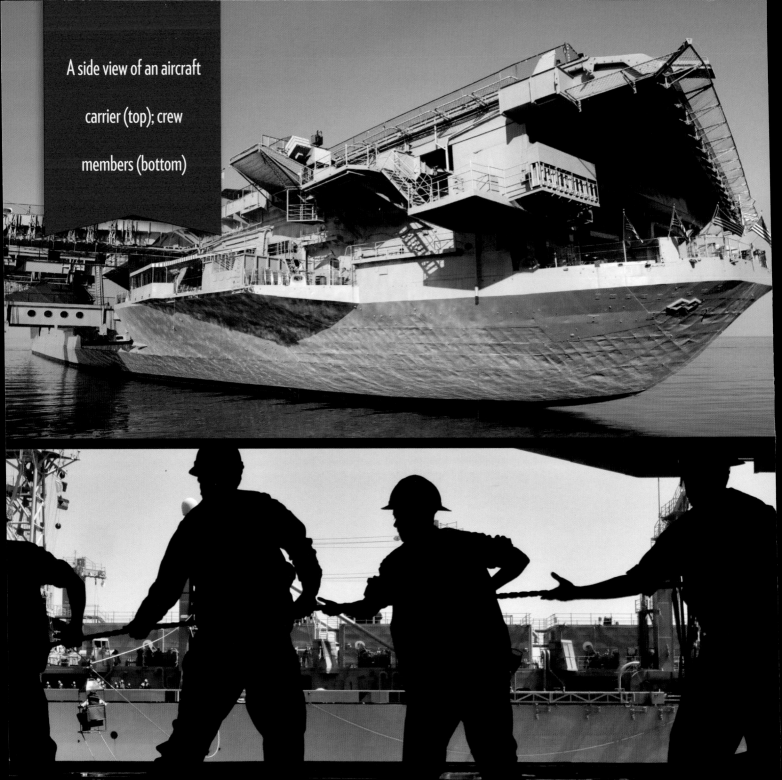

A side view of an aircraft carrier (top); crew members (bottom)

Aircraft carriers have many levels, or decks. The decks have places to sleep, places to eat, and offices for doctors. The hangar deck holds airplanes that are not being used.

The top deck of an aircraft carrier is called the flight deck. A CATAPULT on the runway helps push planes into the air. A wire across the runway catches onto planes to help them stop when they land.

Small, fast planes called jets taking off from an aircraft carrier

U.S. Marines and sailors (left); an aircraft carrier island (right)

A tall tower called the island rises up from the flight deck. This is where the captain controls the ship.

Aircraft carriers can have up to 6,000 crew members! The crew members live on the ship for many months at a time. They sleep in crowded rooms.

★ Famous Aircraft Carrier ★
Nimitz Class

COUNTRY

United States

ENTERED SERVICE

1975

LENGTH

1,092 feet (333 m)

WIDTH

134 feet (40.8 m)

WEIGHT

97,000 tons (87,997 t)

FASTEST SPEED

36 miles (58 km) per hour

CREW

5,680

Nimitz class aircraft carriers are the biggest carriers in the world! They run on a special kind of energy called NUCLEAR POWER. They can stay at sea for years at a time.

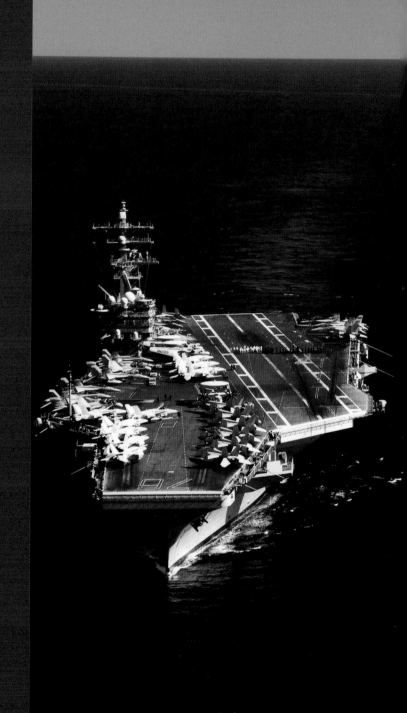

When an aircraft carrier goes into battle, airplanes roar down its runway. The airplanes drop bombs or fire guns and MISSILES (*MIS-sulz*) at the enemy. Other ships with weapons sail near the aircraft carrier to protect it.

An aircraft carrier has its own guns and missiles, too. ARMOR protects an aircraft carrier from enemy attacks. It keeps the aircraft carrier safe to fight another day!

A fighter jet (top);

missile (bottom left);

bombs (bottom right)

Charles de Gaulle

COUNTRY

France

ENTERED SERVICE

2001

LENGTH

858 feet (261.5 m)

WIDTH

103 feet (31.4 m)

WEIGHT

37,085 tons (33,643 t)

FASTEST SPEED

31 miles (50 km) per hour

CREW

1,950

The *Charles de Gaulle* (*GAHL*) has equipment that keeps its flight deck steady in high waves. The ship has a narrow bottom and wider top. This shape makes it hard for enemy RADAR to find it.

The *Charles de Gaulle* (bottom) sailing with other ships

GLOSSARY

armor—a layer of metal and other strong materials that covers a military vehicle and protects it from attacks

catapult—a machine that is built onto the runway on an aircraft carrier; it is attached to a bar on the front of an airplane and helps the airplane take off by pulling it down the runway fast

missiles—exploding weapons that are pushed through the air by rockets to hit a target

nuclear power—a type of energy created when tiny parts of certain kinds of metals split apart

patrol—to move back and forth through an area to protect it

radar—a system that uses radio waves and computers to find objects such as enemy ships

INDEX

WEB SITES

Navy News Service: Aircraft Carriers Photo Gallery http://www.navy.mil/view_gallery.asp?category_id=10 See pictures of U.S. aircraft carriers in action.

Super Coloring: Military Coloring Pages http://www.supercoloring.com/pages/category/military/ Print and color pictures of all your favorite military machines.

READ MORE

Demarest, Chris. *Alpha, Bravo, Charlie: The Military Alphabet*. New York: Margaret K. McElderry Books, 2005.

Zobel, Derek. *Nimitz Aircraft Carriers*. Minneapolis: Torque Books, 2009.